Chocolate Obsession

Chocolate Caramel Vanilla, Volume 3

Shaun J. Phree

Published by PLE Press LLC, 2021.

Also by Shaun J. Phree

Chocolate Caramel Vanilla
Caramel Addiction
Vanilla Fetish
Chocolate Obsession

Nu Delta Chi Series
My Bruh's Keeper

Nu Nu Lambda Series
Soror Love
Soror Fear

Standalone
No Love Lost: A Poetic Tale
10 Steps to Self Care
Her Mother, My Love

Never
Between Seconds
Writer's Surge
Classified

CHAPTER ONE

Rose petals danced on top of the water complying with the waves Lexi's body created in the bath. The pale pink fogged water filled with oils washed away the stress of the day and returned her skin to its supple radiant resting place. She watched the milk-filled water drip down her thighs. She smiled, thinking of her lover in the next room.

"I have to run an errand; I'll be back in 30 minutes." Persia stuck her head into the bathroom, inhaling the peppermint-infused air. *Smells so good.*

"Don't make me wait all night for you," Lexi shot Persia a look she knew all too well. Persia kissed her on the forehead.

"I'll see you in a bit." Persia walked out of the bathroom. Lexi listened for the front door closing.

THE ELEVATOR DOORS opened to her floor. The sanitized white color everywhere made her feel uneasy. Her body told her to go back home, but she couldn't; *Lexi was right; I can't just end it without at least a conversation.* She gathered her strength and stepped out of the elevator. She slowly approached Ashli's room, scanning for any visitors that were familiar.

Ashli's eyes lit up like a Christmas tree. She was alone, which caught Persia off guard. It seemed like no matter what she thought, she couldn't stop feeling this strongly about Ashli.

"I didn't think you were coming back," Ashli whispered.

"Neither did I," Persia confessed.

"Where's Lexi?" She knew the answer but needed to hear the words.

"She's at home," Persia had to tell Lexi the truth when she made it home. She didn't want Lexi to come with her. She had to do this on her own.

"You come to see me without the wife? I may have a chance after all." Ashli saw the sadness in Persia's eyes.

"Ashli, I wanted us to talk alone," Persia responded. "You lied to me. You know how I feel about lying."

"I know," Ashli sighed.

"You and I have been so great. Why didn't you tell me the truth?" Persia asked.

"I knew you'd leave me. You're the only one who sees me, knows me. I couldn't lose you," she hung her head in shame.

"I would have always been here for you. I can't have that type of darkness in our interactions. You're not the only one I was sharing energy with. Damn it, Ashli, you know how protective I am about our links. They have to be pure. Even after I told you about Jade and that bullshit. You still didn't tell me the truth." Persia was visibly disgusted. Ashli and Persia had a long conversation before they started interacting. Persia was truly clear about her expectations. No lying at the top of her list.

"I don't know," Ashli responded. "I just couldn't lose you. I didn't know what else to do."

"Ashli baby, you and I are done. I wish you would have said something," Persia paced the room. "We can stay friends, but that's it. I can't risk it."

"I know, Persia," she sighed again. "It's okay. I'm staying with Brian. He loves me, and I'm having a baby."

"You're having his baby?" Persia inquired.

"I don't know. I really don't know. I had an affair before Brian, and I went to see his parents. It could be his...Richard." Tears flowed down her cheeks. "But Brian doesn't care. He wants to be with us and take care of us."

Persia read Ashli's face. She didn't want to marry Brian, but she decided it was time to settle. She'd created too much drama in everyone else's life. She couldn't ruin her baby's life, even if she never wanted it.

"That's good. Congratulations, I hope you two are happy together." Persia responded.

"I'm in love with you, Persia. I always have been." She was sure it wouldn't make a difference. She needed to be honest.

"I love you too, Ashli. We just don't fit together anymore." Persia kissed Ashli on the forehead. Ashli didn't respond. Persia walked towards the door; she paused and turned to look at Ashli. She smiled at Persia and blew her one last kiss. Persia returned the smile and walked out the door.

That was the last time Ashli saw Persia. She called to congratulate her on her new baby after the birth. She sent her a gift. That was the extent of their friendship from then on. They remained holiday card friends, only contacting each other during birthdays and holidays.

CHAPTER TWO

Persia smiled at her chocolate queen wrapped in what looked like clouds. Lexi was lying in their king-sized bed wrapped in white linen.

"Lexi?" Persia whispered to see if Lexi was awake. Lexi didn't respond. Persia snuck up on the side of the bed to scare Lexi, but she got a surprise herself. Lexi jumped up and grabbed Persia, slamming her on the bed.

"Aghhhh!" Lexi screamed, tickling her in a frenzy.

"Get off me!" Persia yelled, laughing.

"I told you not to make me wait. Where were you?" Lexi asked. Persia sat up, and a serious look poured over her face.

"I went to see Ashli. That's why it took so long. I was ending it with her." Persia held Lexi's hand in hers. "I'm sorry for not explaining that before I left. I needed to do this by myself. It went well, and it's over," Persia finished.

"How did she take it?" Lexi asked.

"She knew it was coming, so she took it well." Persia stared down at the end of the bed. Her heart ached for her lost lover. Their relationship was more than just sex. They had a connection Persia hadn't found with anyone else. She had to release it.

Lexi lifted Persia's head by her chin and looked at her, "You're allowed to mourn the loss. She meant something to you. I know you. We all mean so much to you."

"...and losing any of you is heartbreaking," Persia assured her. "I'll be fine." Lexi gently kissed Persia on her nose.

"I have a surprise for you. You won't get it until your birthday," Lexi teased.

"My birthday. That's a month away. Why are you telling me now?" Persia asked.

"So, it will drive you up a wall for a month," Lexi burst into laughter. Persia gave Lexi an unhappy look. If she were capable, Persia would have burned a hole through Lexi's head. Lexi loved it, and it showed. "Anyway, you owe me something, right?"

"Is that right?" Persia pulled Lexi towards her on the bed. She quickly flipped Lexi over onto her stomach. "I can't quite remember. What was it again? Dang, I said something to you before I left. I can't remember."

Lexi quickly started to show her irritation with her body movements. Persia attempted to keep Lexi on her stomach, but she knew she wouldn't last long.

"Try me," Lexi dared Persia, looking over her shoulder.

Persia silently accepted the challenge. She ran her tongue, tracing Lexi's thighs up to her ass. She kissed and licked each cheek, then ran her tongue between them. Lexi's body squirmed with pleasure and anticipation. She wasn't good at being teased. Persia parted her ass and legs, revealing the stream flowing onto the bed. Lexi arched her back slightly. She could hear Persia's belt clinking behind her, signaling her what to expect next. To her surprise, Persia's tongue explored between her cheeks, causing her to release a soft moan, and then she held her breath. It slid into her over and over, encouraging Lexi to arch her back and open more. She rocked back onto Persia's tongue, burying her fingers into the mattress and her screams into her pillow. She froze. Her movements, the rocking, it stopped. Her body vibrated so quickly it was almost unnoticeable. Persia knew better than to stop. This was the calm before her storm. She gripped Lexi's thighs and braced herself. The tension released from Lexi's body, her chest fell to the bed, she screamed into the pillow, and she came. Persia laid on top of Lexi, kissing her neck, which resulted in weak moans. Lexi reached between her legs and guided Persia's strap into her. It struggled to stay in her, fighting against her flood. She pressed against it slowly but hard. She quickly arched her back again and settled on her knees with her chest still glued to the bed. Persia, behind her, held on to her hips while she enjoyed the view. Lexi didn't let out a sound, but her nails dug into the covers, and her body shivered. Persia kept going, faster. Lexi matched her speed and then increased it.

"Oh, Shit, No!" Lexi screamed before exploding. She pushed Persia's strap out of her and squirted everywhere. "Fuck...damn baby."

"Babe?" Persia said. No response. Just silence. "Damn, she sleep already."

Persia got up and got ready for bed. She looked at Lexi laying in their bed and was filled with love and adoration. Her mind wandered to Ashli. Missing her was hitting harder than she expected. A couple of tears fell, the last tears she'd shed for Ashli.

CHAPTER THREE

"Moving on up to the monogamous side, in that deluxe condo in the sky!" Karen started singing, walking down the hallway to Persia's office.

"Bro, don't come in here with that shit. I told you I'm not monogamous." Persia contested.

"You got a woman?" Karen asked.

"Yeah, but..." Persia rolled her eyes.

"And only one?" Karen chuckled.

"Shut the fuck up K! I lost two that doesn't mean I'm mono. You know that." Persia was visibly irritated.

"And you are in a deluxe condo on a high floor?" Karen waited for the response.

"You a fool. You right. Still not monogamous." Persia laughed. "But we are one on one."

"Exactly, going off on me and shit like I'm wrong," Karen responded. "Fuck you, bro. You got that confusing ass life."

"I'm not having this conversation with you." Persia flipped Karen off. Karen and Persia maintained their friendship by staying honest with each other. "You always fucking with me."

"You shouldn't be so touchy. That's the life you live. You already know everyone has something to say about it." Karen looked at Persia seriously. "I'm only coming at you with love, fam, always."

"I know, I got you. It hurts," Persia said.

"I know, bro. You haven't been talking to me, so I figured I'd irritate you until you speak up. I knew you'd spill it eventually." Karen winked at Persia.

"You think you're slick. I didn't realize you were smart," Persia jabbed.

"That's smart. You mean you didn't think I was THAT smart." Karen nodded, waiting for Persia to agree with her. "Right?"

"Uh, yeah, whatever you say," Persia chuckled. One of her most important clients was walking towards her office. "You gotta go. Cason is coming."

"Fuck you, we will finish this shit later," Karen whispered, exiting Persia's office.

"Mr. Cason, how are you today?" Persia stood up to greet him.

"Persia, how many times do I have to tell you to call me Don," he responded.

"Sorry about that, Mr..." Persia laughed. "Don."

"Do you have the Gibson file for me?" Don asked.

"Here you go. Are we still on for our meeting next week?" Persia inquired.

"Absolutely," Don responded.

"Great, I'm looking forward to this article," Persia smiled.

"I'll see you next week. Bring a few new ideas with you." Don scooped up the file and headed out the door.

Persia waved at Don as he exited her office. She sat down in her chair, smiling. She worked extremely hard to make moves in her company.

Karen slipped back into Persia's office. "You're really trying to make this move, huh?"

"Where the hell did you come from?" Persia was startled.

"Waiting on Mr. Cason to leave. Back to you and the new wife. Are you inviting another one?" Karen plopped down on the couch in Persia's office. "Do you need another one?"

"You been here long enough. I can't go looking for anyone. Things will work out the way it should. For now, Lexi and I are enjoying each other," Persia said.

"Shut up, P. You already have someone on the hook." The two burst into laughter.

"I don't really have time or the mindset to date someone new right now. I lost Jade not too long ago, and now Ashli. It's time to grieve the losses and then move forward." Persia looked sad. "I can't put any past shit on a new woman. That's not right."

"Yeah, you're right. Especially with this many women being involved." Karen noticed Persia's attention was drawn to her computer screen. "What's up?"

"I just got this weird ass email." Persia pointed at her screen and continued, "Read this shit, bro."

Karen walked behind Persia's desk and read the email over her shoulder.

Happiness isn't for you.
You will endure great loss.
Change your ways
Or suffer the consequences.

"What in the fake ass horoscope is this shit. Is that Lexi?" Karen stared, turning red. "...this is a threat!"

Persia was dialing her work phone, ignoring Karen.

"Where are you?" Persia huffed into the phone. "Stay there; I'm coming to pick you up."

"You have a meeting in 30 minutes," Karen whispered, pointing to the calendar on her desk.

"Shit. I have a meeting, I forgot. Karen will come pick you up," she said while waiting for a nod from Karen. She agreed. "Text me the address. Don't worry about your car. WE will pick it up later."

Persia hung up and turned her attention to Karen. "Thank you, fam. I just texted you the address. Bring her here."

"I got you. I got you," She headed out the door.

Time passed quickly while Persia was in her meeting. She barely paid attention to work, just the clock ticking away slowly. She waited to see Karen walk through the hallways to signal her they were back or a vibration from her phone giving bad news. She maintained her focus on her presentation. She rarely showed tension at work. Her phone vibrated in her pocket, and she paused.

"Persia? Are you okay?" a grey-haired man at the table asked.

"Yes, I'm fine. My apologies. Furthermore..." she continued her presentation with ease. She knew the vibration was Karen.

"WHAT IS GOING ON?" Lexi rushed at Persia when she walked into her office. She buried her face into Persia's neck, and her heartbeat was slowing down. "Is anyone going to tell me what is going on?"

"I got a weird email with a photo of you, talking about consequences if I don't change my ways. I thought someone was going to hurt you." Persia caressed Lexi's face between her hands. Staring her in the eyes, "Are you okay?"

"I'm fine. You scared me." Lexi hugged Persia again. "I'm okay. Do you know who sent it?"

"No, it came from an anonymous email address. It's untraceable," Karen responded. "I already checked."

Persia shook Karen's hand in gratitude. "We are going to lay low for a while. Just until I figure out if this is serious or not."

"Ok, baby. I can move everything around for the next couple of weeks. I'll schedule phone and video conferences instead. What about you? You can't get around coming to work." Lexi looked at Persia and then at Karen, waiting for one of them to answer. No one did. Karen sat on the couch, and Persia settled in her desk chair. Both with no ideas. "It seems like you will have to come to work, and I will be at home."

"No, I'm taking off. I will work from home a few days a week, and I'll come in the other two days a week. Karen will help keep an eye on you. Right?" Persia waited for Karen's response.

"You know it, P. I got you, Lexi. I'll even cook you up one of my special meals." Karen smiled.

"Girl, you know you can't cook." Lexi laughed. Her beautiful smile lit up the room and lightened Persia's heavy, worrying heart. "Feel better, baby?"

"Yes, I do," Persia responded. She wrapped her arms around Lexi's waist and pulled her in. Softly kissing her between words, she said, "I... Love... You... Too... Much... To... Lose... You."

"Y'all make me sick. I'm out. I'll see you tomorrow, Lex. P, keep that shit in here." Karen walked out of the office, throwing up the peace sign.

"She jealous," Persia whispered.

"I don't think she is," Lexi laughed. She pulled out her phone and showed Persia photos of Karen with three different women. "And that was just on the way back here to your office."

"Damn, she is pulling them like that. I might need to..." Persia felt Lexi's eyes burning a hole in her head.

"...go ahead. Finish that sentence. You might need to what?" Lexi pulled back and waited for the answer.

"I might need to talk to her about settling down. It's done me right." Persia kissed Lexi.

"Yeah, you do need to speak to her. Speaking of, will you want another lover?" Lexi asked.

"I don't know. With everything that has happened. I don't want to look for anything. Let's take things slow and enjoy our time together. Whatever happens, we will handle it when it comes up," Persia responded.

"Fair enough. I'm just asking. There are a lot of beautiful women out here," Lexi said.

"There is no beauty out there that is greater than the beauty right here." Persia felt herself growing more in love with Lexi. She didn't think that was possible. Lexi blushed and responded by hugging her lover.

"You and me baby. This is the best team ever," Lexi kissed Persia. "Are you ready to go home?"

"Yes, finally. Let's go home," Persia responded. The two left together and enjoyed their date night. Persia tried hard to put the email out of her mind and Lexi was a good distraction.

CHAPTER FOUR

"Whoa, you can't do that here," Lexi jumped back.

"I just miss you so much, baby," a woman wrapped her arms around Lexi while responding. "I know we will have to end soon."

"Yes, we will. You have your family, the way you wanted it, right?" Lexi caressed the woman's face, "Shamya, right?"

"Yes, I do. I do. He is perfect for us. She loves him, and I have feelings for him now, too. You can't help but fall in love with Kevin." Shamya smiled, thinking about her new lover and enjoying the touches of her soon-to-be past lover.

"See, I told you. Trust me, I know people. He just needed confirmation from you. He was living in a hell of his own making, but no one deserves to be punished like that." Lexi shook her head. Shamya was lost in thought about Kevin. Lexi kissed Shamya and drew her back in. "One more for the road?"

"Egh, that was corny," Shamya responded with disgust.

"Shut up and come here." Lexi grabbed Shamya, but the control reversed quickly. Shamya held her hands in front of her while they kissed. She wouldn't allow Lexi to touch her. Their passionate kisses turned to Shamya's tongue, tracing Lexi's neck, frequently interrupted by gentle bites and sucking. Lexi's thick chocolate thighs rubbed together rhythmically.

"I thought you said not here?" Shamya's voice caused Lexi to open her eyes and remember she was standing in the living room she and Persia shared. This wasn't going to work.

"Follow me." Lexi snatched Shamya's hand and led her out of their apartment. Down every flight of stairs available. Through two concrete doors. Giant pipes and concrete surrounded them. "Scared?"

"You should be." Shamya gripped Lexi's throat in one hand and backed into a steamy room. Still holding Lexi's neck, she pulled down her pants.

Lexi gasped, only letting out small amounts of air and no sound. Her overheating body pressed against the cold concrete wall. The chill quickly broke through her thin tank top. She wasn't wearing a bra. Her leggings were around her ankles, and Shamya's hand was between her legs. She didn't bother to move. Every move only made Shamya's grip on her neck tighter. Lexi came into Shamya's hand and almost lost her balance. Her legs were weakened, and her air was short. Shamya attempted to back up as if she were done. Lexi chuckled and pushed her head down. She lifted one leg over Shamya's shoulder. She got the hint and started feasting. Lexi grabbed the bar above her head to brace herself. She rode Shamya's face to two more orgasms.

"Just one last time?" Shamya's face glistened from her nose to her neck. "You sure?"

"I'm sure," Lexi laughed. She pulled up her leggings and adjusted her clothes. "You are amazing at what you do but you're not worth me losing my Persia."

"You mean you, her, and whoever else. Do you think she will be monogamous with you?" Shamya held back a chuckle.

"Don't be stupid. I'm here with you. I'm not just with her. I know her, and we are meant to be together. Everyone else is optional." Lexi smiled at the joy in Shamya's eyes. She really does love her wife and new boyfriend and is genuinely happy for Lexi. "Just like us."

"You're right. You definitely are not my forever." The two laughed together as they made their way back to the apartment. Shamya didn't stay long. She cleaned up in the bathroom, gathered her things, and said her final goodbyes. "It was fun, Lex."

"It was successful. Send me an invitation to the commitment ceremony." Lexi waved at Shamya as she walked down the hallway.

"Oh, I will. Soon," she responded. "Real soon."

Lexi quickly took a shower, washing away that part of her life. She and Shamya were done. Their relationship served its purpose. Persia walked through the front door shortly after.

CHAPTER FIVE

"**B**aby, it has been a week, and I haven't gone anywhere. We haven't seen anything that even looks like it might be threatening. Can we please go out?" Lexi begged. Persia walked into the living room to find Lexi lying on the couch. "Please?"

Persia stood staring at the beautiful mocha woman laid out in a pink bra and thongs on the couch. She shook her head. "Why are you so damn spoiled?"

"Come taste this pussy and let me remind you." Lexi spread her legs and reached into her panties. She didn't break eye contact with Persia when she put those same fingers in her mouth. Enjoying the taste of herself. "Well?"

"If you get dressed quickly, I'll take you to a movie. I'm already dressed, so you have to hurry," Persia teased. She resisted her hunger. She could have easily lost herself between those legs for the next few hours. Lexi jumped up. She danced across the living room, kissing Persia, then down the hallway to their bedroom.

"Don't tempt me with a good time!" Lexi yelled. She took less than seven minutes to put on jeans, a top, and heels. Another five minutes to freshen up in the bathroom. She put on her favorite lace front wig and touched up her natural makeup. Lip gloss added while she shimmed down the hallway. "I'm done. Let's go."

Persia regretted turning down Lexi's offer. She looked good enough to melt and lick off her fingers. Persia contemplated staying home but was sure Lexi wouldn't let her between her legs if she didn't take her out. No sense in staying home. She grabbed her blazer and Lexi's shawl.

"I saw that thought. I'm glad you reconsidered." Lexi snatched her shawl and stood at the front door.

"I don't know what you mean," Persia laughed. She opened the door, and they headed down the hallway.

In the elevator, Lexi wanted to play. She unbuttoned her shirt one by one. Her breasts fought to break free but were still confined by her bra. She leaned against the elevator wall and unzipped her jeans. Persia glanced at the stop elevator button and then back at Lexi. She had 45 minutes before their movie started. Plenty of time. When she reached for Lexi's jeans, her hand was slapped away.

"No, no, no," Lexi whispered. She stopped the elevator. Persia moved towards her again, but she backed away. "Don't touch, just watch."

Lexi unlatched her bra in the front and played with her already erect nipples. With soft moans, her tongue slid across her lips, sucking her bottom lip. One hand pinching and caressing her nipples, the other slowly up and down in her jeans. Her head fell back, her eyes closed. She wouldn't notice if Persia joined her, but it wasn't often a show like this was offered. The hand in her jeans moved faster. Her breathing shortened. Her eyes opened, focusing on Persia. She whispered oh shit and her body shuddered.

"We are going to miss the movie," Persia faked composure; her soaked boxer briefs would tell on her. Lexi laughed. She knew better than to believe Persia was unaffected. She pulled her hand out of her jeans and put one finger in Persia's mouth. As she expected, Persia licked her finger.

"Get yourself together; we are going to miss the movie." Lexi started the elevator. She pulled two wipes out of her purse and cleaned her hands. The elevator doors opened to their lobby, and Lexi glided towards the front door. Persia slowly followed.

"This is going to be a long night," Persia whispered.

LEXI HAD TALKED ABOUT this romantic comedy frequently since she saw the preview. She was into it. She glanced at Persia from time to time to make sure she wasn't asleep. Her boredom was very apparent, but she didn't complain. Lexi loved that about her. She would act like this was one of the best movies she's seen as long as Lexi was happy.

When the movie was over, Persia went to the restroom. She took a long time. While waiting, Lexi ran into Karen. Lexi and Karen knew each other before Lexi met Persia. The two never were interested in each other, but they maintained a distant friendship to make sure there were clear boundaries once Lexi and Persia became serious. Karen has been a big help since the email threat.

"Are you okay?" Karen asked. "Where is P?"

"She's in the restroom. I'm fine, Karen. Stop worrying about me," Lexi responded. She was grateful to have such a concerned friend.

"OK, well, I just want to make sure you all are cool. I saw you over here alone, and that didn't sit right with me." Karen turned to point at the group she was with. "I know my girl is good with everyone we are with."

"I'm ok, Karen. Persia is right in there," she pointed at the ladies' room. "Go ahead and go back to your girl before she thinks something is going on."

"She knows better than that," Karen reached for a hug. "But alright, I will get back to my group."

As the two broke their embrace they saw Persia standing, watching.

"Hey bro," Karen shook Persia's hand. "I was just about to head back to my girl."

"Glad I caught you," Persia glanced at Lexi and then back at Karen. "Tell your lady I said hello."

"I will. See you later, Lexi." Karen walked back towards her group of friends.

"What was that about?" Persia quickly asked but resumed her composure.

"Nothing, she just saw me standing her alone and wanted to make sure I was ok. After that email, and this being our first time out. She was just...you know," Lexi responded.

"Yeah, things have been chaotic lately," she held Lexi's hand. "Let's go."

They walked through the lobby, and Lexi was in bliss. She didn't care about where they were or what they were doing. As long as they were out the house together she was happy. They spent too much time couped up in their apartment. The parking lot was half full and quiet.

"What do you want for dinner?" Lexi asked Persia. "We can stop for something, or I can cook for you?"

"Let's get something delivered. I want to get back home." Persia wrapped her arms around Lexi, spun her around, and hugged her. She was just about to get lost in her sweet aroma when a light caught the corner of her eye. Screeching tires, smoke, and lights lit up the corner of the parking lot. Someone was coming towards them and fast. Fear didn't creep through until Persia saw the light bounce off the gun. "OH FUCK!"

The sound of bullets rang out across the parking lot. Persia swung Lexi back around and towards the door. She fell into the theater lobby door onto the floor. Persia jumped on the ground. The car tires screeched again, and it disappeared around the corner. Lexi leaped off the ground of the theater and rushed out the door. She searched for Persia. She was sitting in a corner against the wall.

"I don't think we will make it for our food delivery, baby," Persia looked down at her side, where blood filled her shirt and started pooling on the ground. Lexi screamed; she wrapped her shawl up and put pressure on Persia's wound.

"You'll be ok, baby. You'll be ok. I'm going to…" Lexi dialed 911 on her cell phone. She cried and gave every bit of information she could to the dispatcher. She heard the ambulance sirens within minutes. "…you hear them baby. They are here for you. I told you. It's going to be ok."

Persia smiled. "I love you."

"Stop that. I love you too, but you're going to be ok," Lexi cried. A guy handed Lexi his shirt and told her to press harder. "I'm trying!"

Persia leaned her head back and closed her eyes. She was so tired. She just needed to rest a bit.

"Baby, no! You have to wake up; here they come." Lexi rubbed her face, then she tapped her cheek a bit, but she didn't respond. "Baby? Baby, please wake up...Persia!"

CHAPTER SIX

Soft needle pains roamed Persia's body, but she couldn't feel much except for the tube in her throat. The scent of vanilla engulfed the air around her. The covers around her were tightly tucked into the sides of the bed; her fingers searched for anything other than the sheets. Soft chatter in the distance; she was distracted by the constant beeping noise. Her body began to release itself back into sleep, but her mind overpowered it.

"Well, if it isn't ole sleeping beast finally waking up," a familiar voice joked; her eyes searched the room. A brown-skinned, slender woman straddled her on the bed. "Are you going to keep me waiting, or are you going to look at me?"

Her chapped lips spread into a small smile at her best friend hanging over her. Her hair framed their tunnel as they stared at each other. She kissed Persia on the forehead, "I'm glad you are alive, asshole."

"Excuse me!" Lexi startled the two. "What...Baby! You're awake!" She rushed to Persia, and the brown-skinned woman didn't move. "Can you get off my woman?"

"Oh shit, Lexi. My bad. Nice to meet you," the androgynously dressed woman climbed off the hospital bed and extended her hand. "Robin. I'm Robin."

"Hmph, Robin, nice to meet you." Lexi searched her mind for the name and found a memory of Persia telling her about her best friend from high school, Robin. Her first love turned lifetime best friend. She reluctantly shook her hand. "She... woke up for you?"

"It's been forever since we've seen each other." Robin smiled at Persia. "Just call me Rob."

"Thank you for coming...Rob. You woke my baby up." The nurse came in and asked them to leave. She had to remove the tube and check Persia's vitals. When they returned, Persia was sitting up a bit. The nurse warned them to take it easy.

"So, how about drinks tonight?" Rob joked.

"Shut the fuck up," Persia whispered. Lexi was caught off guard. She'd only heard Persia talk to her masculine friends like that, but Robin looked very feminine. Her skinny-fit ripped jeans, tank top, and Jordan's were pretty typical. She wore a long, straight, red, and black weave; Lexi frequently caught herself lost in the red strands dancing on Rob's breasts. A big difference from Lexi's lace, pink, and soft attire.

"Get ya ass up and make me..." Rob crossed her arms and checked her watch. "Right, that's what I thought. Now, can someone explain to me how preppy boi, here, got shot?"

Persia looked up at Lexi as the tears started to gather in her eyes. Rob read the room. The hurt and guilt filled it, suffocating the words out of all three of them. Rob plopped down on the limp excuse for a couch. Persia reached for Lexi's hand. She couldn't express herself verbally; she squeezed her hand.

"How long?" Persia whispered.

"Three days Papi. You've been sleeping for three long days. The doctors said you will recover. The bullet went straight through. You lost... a lot of blood," Lexi fought the lump in her throat. She could feel Persia squeezing her hand tighter. She had to be strong. "Everything is okay. See, I told you. You will be fine."

Persia turned to Rob, searching for a hint that Lexi wasn't telling the truth. Rob didn't flinch. She really was going to be ok. Reaching for the table, she whispered, "Water."

"Bro, you need some Hennessey. Forget water," Rob laughed. Persia weakly flipped her off. "I'm just saying, have you jumping out this bed and back on this beautiful, chocolate treat right here."

A soft hint of red burst through Lexi's cheeks as her smile spread across her face, "That's what I'm waiting for..." she seductively glanced at Persia.

"Shit, if I were you, bro, I would be counting the minutes," Rob flashed a smile at Lexi.

"Get off my woman," Persia laughed softly.

"I'm not on her...yet..." Rob slid off the couch and stood next to Lexi. "...but if you're stingy..."

Lexi watched the looks between Persia and Rob. They seemed to have an entire conversation in the shifting of their eyes. Persia didn't seem to agree at first, but her glare quickly softened, "As I'm here in my hospital bed."

"We got you, bro. You will always be good." Rob laughed, wrapping her arm around Lexi's waist and drawing her in. Lexi grew tense against Rob's body; her hand slowly fell to her hip. Rob pecked Lexi on the cheek. Persia reassured Lexi by caressing her hand; she saw Lexi searching her face for direction.

"I have always been good because of both of you. Thanks for coming, Rob." Persia felt tears filling her eyes; she fought them. "Maybe I do need that drink."

The three of them burst into laughter, a relief to Lexi. The growing moisture between her thighs was making her increasingly uncomfortable. Rob's soft glances, strong grip, and sweet, vanilla scent intrigued Lexi. Her mind drifted to her fingers in Rob's hair and her legs around her neck...to ride her tongue. She was different. Persia had a soft masculinity and quiet dominance that allowed Lexi to submit fully to her. Rob, on the other hand, was all feminine...except for her grip. Usually, Lexi was more dominant than the femmes she interacted with. She pushed the thought out of her head. *What was she thinking? Rob is Persia's best friend...her first love. Persia is in a hospital bed.*

"How long do you have to stay in here?" Rob asked. "I love you, but I can't do this hospital shit."

"The nurse said she'll be ready to go home tomorrow, hopefully. Are you leaving?" Lexi gave a subtle pout.

Rob chuckled, "No, I have a room for a while."

"You're staying?" Persia confirmed.

"Do you want me to leave?" Rob responded. "I thought you were raised with more manners than that?

"Shut up. You're staying at the house." Persia nodded towards Lexi. "I need someone to stay with her while I'm here anyway."

"I'm not going any-fucking-where." Lexi crossed her arms. "I've been here since you have, and I'm not going until you do."

"Go home for a few hours and rest in our bed. You are starting to look tired." Persia knew that would get under her skin.

"Tir..." Lexi glared at Persia and bit her bottom lip. "...whatever you say," Lexi flipped Persia off.

Rob jumped up and hugged Lexi from behind. Her small breasts and hard nipples pressed into Lexi's back. Her breathing deepened. She must have blinked too slowly a couple of times.

"Are you okay?" Persia poked Lexi's thigh.

"Yes, Papi, I'm fine." Lexi regained her composure. "Rob just smells so sweet all against me."

Rob kissed her neck. Looking at Persia, she whispered into Lexi's ear, "Probably not as sweet as you."

The uncomfortable, aroused feeling returned stronger than before. Lexi didn't know how to respond or if she should. So, she just rolled her eyes. It was unlike Lexi to stumble in her actions. Rob really threw her off her balance.

"How about you take me back to your place and let me get settled in? You can take a shower, change clothes, and be back here within a couple of hours." Rob continued. "Do you have an extra bedroom?"

"Lexi? Can you set her up at the house, and you can come right back?" Persia agreed.

Lexi was reluctant but didn't know how to explain why she couldn't. It was better if she went along with it. Maybe it was all just in her head, and Rob was messing with her.

"Fine, but I will be right back. I'll shower, change, then right back here." Lexi had a stern expression.

Persia weakly threw her hands in the air in compliance with a sarcastic grin. Lexi responded with her middle finger. Rob grabbed her overnight bag and headed towards the hospital room door.

"I'll be out front," Rob stated to the room and signaled she needed to grab a smoke. She blew Persia a kiss and headed out. "See you soon."

"Aight bro." Persia responded. She looked back at Lexi, "Go ahead, baby. The sooner you get out of here, the sooner you can get back to me."

"Ok. Here's your call button and the remote. If you need anything don't be afraid to make them earn their pay," Lexi laughed.

"I love you, Lex. Bye." Persia kissed Lexi and waved her off. She turned over to get some rest as Lexi left the room.

CHAPTER SEVEN

The keys fumbled in Lexi's hands as she tried to unlock the front door of her apartment with Rob hovering over her. Her sweet vanilla aroma slowed Lexi's movements, her eyes rolled back into her head and closed, and she gently leaned back onto Rob. Rob cleared her throat with a smile.

"Shit," Lexi sighed. She shook her head and focused on her keys. Rob didn't back up; she leaned in closer. The door opened, and the two of them stumbled into the apartment. "Girl?"

"My bad, Lex." Rob chuckled and walked past Lexi into their living room. "Nice place."

"Thanks," Lexi smiled. "It's our sanctuary."

"Was this your place or hers?" Rob threw her duffle on the couch and flipped off her Jordan's.

"It's our place." Lexi left Rob alone in the living room and went into her bedroom. She opened her underwear drawer, pulled out two pairs of underwear, matching bras, and threw them on the bed. She walked into her closet to find an outfit for today and something to change into tomorrow. Irritated at Rob, she forgot she was there. She pulled off her clothes, standing in only her lilac lace bra and thong set. She swayed back into her bedroom and tossed the two outfits on the bed with her underwear. Her attention was caught by her appearance in her door-sized mirror. She rubbed her smooth chocolate skin from her breasts to her stomach and her hips, admiring her thick figure.

"Nice view, huh?" Rob leaned on the door of her bedroom, smiling seductively. Lexi spun around in surprise but didn't cover herself; she put her hands on her hips.

"What the hell are you doing in here?" Lexi frowned. "You're supposed to be in the living room."

"I was coming to ask you where your wine glasses are, but now I'm enjoying the view." Rob slowly entered the room. "Are you uncomfortable?"

"Do I look like I'm uncomfortable?" Lexi flipped Rob off. "Get the hell out so I can finish and get back to my baby."

"She's sleep. You saw her when we left. She will be out for hours. Give her a chance to get some rest." Rob was sitting on the bed next to Lexi's pile of clothes.

"How did 'get out', turn into you sitting on my bed," Lexi said. She grabbed Rob's arm and pulled her to her feet.

"Damn," Rob licked her bottom lip with Lexi's hand wrapped around her arm. "Are you going to let me go?"

"Get out!" Lexi shoved Rob towards the door. "You're crossing all types of lines."

Rob stumbled to gain her balance. "Don't play me, Lex; I know Persia. If you're with her, I know you too. And lines is something y'all don't do in the traditional sense." Rob chuckled.

"You don't know me, Robin." Lexi's emphasis on her name shot flames between Rob's legs, and she bit her bottom lip. Lexi noticed. She stalled before making her next statement. "...are you hitting on me?"

Rob took a couple of slow steps toward Lexi, "Are you interested?"

Lexi's full lips parted the slightest bit, but enough for Rob to see her arousal. She took a couple more steps towards Lexi, waiting for a response.

"Well?" she asked.

"I'M TIRED, ROBIN. I just want to take a shower, put on fresh, comfortable clothes, and get back to the hospital. Can I do that?" Lexi responded. Rob's forehead wrinkled, and her jaw tightened. Before she knew it, Lexi dropped her head in submission but quickly raised it again. Rob was standing less than a foot away from her. She could feel her breath. Attempting to distract from her brief moment of submission, Lexi gestured towards the door and asked, "Can I?"

"Sure, Lex," Rob responded but didn't move. Instead, she leaned in toward Lexi, making her breath deepen. Lexi's full mocha breasts were tightly contained by her bra and moved up and down. Rob's eyes moved in unison as her tongue ran across her bottom lip. "Do you need any help?"

Lexi didn't respond. She just lowered her eyes and stayed still. She could feel the cool metal from Rob's jeans pressed against her stomach. Rob reached around to Lexi's back and ran the tip of her fingers up her spine to her bra. She snapped her fingers and Lexi's bra released. She traced her fingertip to Lexi's shoulder and dragged her bra strap down her arms, freeing her full dark nipples. Lexi closed her eyes when Rob's thumb grazed her nipple, sending chills through her body. Then nothing. Rob wasn't pressed against her; she didn't feel her touch or hear her breathing. She quickly opened her eyes to find Rob picking up her towel.

"Here you go," she handed Lexi the body towel. "Enjoy your shower."

"Th...Thanks," Lexi was confused and relieved. The puddle forming in her thongs wasn't going to stay there for long. "I'm going to shower. There's plenty of food in the fridge. The glasses are in the cabinet above the dishwasher. Get settled in."

"I will," Rob smiled. Lexi paused for a moment, hoping Rob would take the chance, but she didn't. Lexi turned around and walked towards the bathroom.

Rob left the bedroom and walked into the living room. Everything inside her wanted to turn around and make love to Lexi in the shower. She knew she and Persia never had issues about things like this. They also never went through one of them almost dying. This probably isn't the best time. Rob opened her duffle and pulled out her blunt holder. She popped it open, pulled out two blunts, and shoved the holder back into the bag. She searched her pants and her jacket for a lighter, it fell on the floor. She laid her body across the couch, lit one blunt, and tossed the other on the end table. She didn't bother to open her eyes while she smoked, except to get rid of the ash. She put her first blunt out and still heard the shower running. She shook her head, trying to shake the thought of her and Lexi. She reached over to the end table and grabbed her second blunt. Might as well get comfortable. She lit it. True to her pattern, she laid back, closed her eyes, and let her mind drift into the smoke. She lay a little too long and realized she had probably dropped her ashes, but she smelled the sweetness in the air. She opened her eyes to

Lexi standing over her, a towel wrapped around her head, and another wrapped around her dripping wet body.

"What the fuck are you doing?" Lexi raised her voice.

"You said get settled in. This is me settling in. You don't smoke in the house? I know Persia smokes." Rob sat up and started waving at the smoke in the air.

"We don't smoke out here. Either on the patio or in our office." Lexi pointed towards a door down the hallway. "You really could have asked instead of focusing on taking off my bra."

"You're still thinking about that huh?" Rob smirked. She rubbed up the inside of Lexi's thigh until she was stopped where they met. Lexi smiled. Rob didn't back down. Lexi parted her thighs, inviting Rob to keep going. Her hand settled between Lexi's thighs rubbing her hairless lips. She was already wet when Rob started teasing her clit. Lexi released soft moans.

"I need help with releasing some of the stress. Do you think you can lend a..." Lexi licked her lips.

"...a tongue, finger or two? I think I can help." Rob responded while watching Lexi remove her towel and lay with her legs open on the couch. She reached for the blunt and took two deep hits, she held it, then slowly released very little smoke. She repeated the cycle one more time before putting the blunt in the ashtray and lying back on the couch. Rob's eyes took in the entire view. She didn't waste any time before running her tongue between Lexi's pussy lips. Lexi attempted to hold her stomach, but Rob brushed her hands away. She caressed Lexi's voluptuous body, enjoying every inch of her. She licked circles around her clit and continued to indulge in Lexi for twenty minutes. Lexi came twice before she pushed Rob away from her. She tried to close her legs, but Rob resisted. Instead, she slid up Lexi's body. She wrapped Lexi's legs around her waist and kissed her.

"Feel better?" Rob asked, kissing Lexi's neck.

"So much better." Lexi enjoyed the attention. It was different for her to be wrapped up with such a beautiful feminine woman. It was a needed change. "Now I really have to shower and get back to the hospital."

"Lex, you really should try to take a quick nap. Jump in the shower and then lay down for a couple of hours." Rob saw the disagreement on Lexi's face, so she continued, "You know Persia will be sleep for at least 3 or 4 more hours."

"She was really tired....and so am I," Lexi complied reluctantly. "...but I'm setting my alarm. Two hours, that's it."

"Ok. Two hours." Lexi got up and collected her towels. Rob slapped her ass and watched. "Damn."

"Watch yourself. Don't get too comfortable." Lexi frowned at Rob and walked into her bedroom. She closed the door. Rob heard the bedroom door lock. She smirked.

I might as well get a nap, too. Rob lit her blunt and laid back on the couch. She finished smoking and fell asleep.

CHAPTER EIGHT

Persia was up watching TV by the time Lexi returned to the hospital. She hoped Lexi had a chance to relax; the last few days had to be hectic for her. Persia barely slept more than an hour at a time because of her nightmares. She couldn't remember exactly what happened, but she was getting flashes in her dreams. Bits and pieces. Just enough to drive her out of her mind while she was awake. She needed to know who shot her. What happened?

"I'm back," Lexi announced, entering the hospital room. "Looks like you're awake already. I thought you were supposed to be getting some sleep too?"

"I try when I can," Persia responded quietly. "How was your rest? Do you feel better?"

"I feel refreshed, thank you." Lexi kissed Persia and lingered on her lips for a moment.

"Did Rob help you relax?" Persia asked with a smirk on her face. Something wasn't quite right with that question, but Lexi wasn't sure how to respond.

"How was she supposed to help me, Persia?" Realizing she may have been set up, Lexi started her own interrogation. Persia just laughed softly. "No, no... go ahead. I'm listening."

"I know Rob, and I know her type. Are you mad at me?" Persia didn't answer the question.

"Why would I be mad at you? You haven't said you did anything." Lexi played dumb. She gave Persia a sharp look, waiting for her answer.

"I knew Rob would go after you. She thinks you're sexy. When I pushed you to take her home, I figured she'd try to push up on you." Persia confessed.

"You set me up to have sex with your best friend?" Lexi asked.

"I didn't set you up. I was just hoping you'd get a chance to relax. A chance I can't give you right now." Persia looked down at her body in the hospital bed.

"Hmph," Lexi pressed her lips together. "It was actually me that came on to her."

"Oh, so you weren't so worried about me in here, huh?" Persia messed with Lexi.

"Shut up." Lexi slapped Persia's leg. "I needed a release, and she served the purpose."

"You're welcome. You look much better." Persia took credit.

"I'm not thanking you. Don't set me up. Had me going crazy in my head, making sure I wasn't crossing a line or something." Lexi said. She sat on the edge of Persia's hospital bed and held her hand. "But yes, I did need to relax a bit."

"Baby, I'm not worried about you. I know where you belong, and so do you. Rob is my best friend, and she knows how I am almost better than anyone else. I trust she wouldn't cross a line I wasn't comfortable with. I also know how talented her tongue is." Persia smiled.

"Shit, it is. She did some things to me I haven't experienced," Lexi said with a shiver. "She's just so little."

"She's always been little and strong. Did you two get a chance to talk and get to know each other?" Persia asked.

"Not really. I took a shower. She made me cum, and then I went to sleep." Lexi shrugged her shoulders. "I didn't really have time for that. She was lighting up in our living room, though. I guess you could say she got to know me a little better when I snapped off on her."

"Babe, really?" Persia laughed.

Rob strolled into the hospital room moving slowly with low eyes. She smiled at Persia and tossed a bag on the bed.

"You're welcome, asshole." Rob landed on the couch. She threw her head back.

"I knew you'd get me something to eat." Persia opened the greasy bag and pulled out a giant cheeseburger dripping with all the fixings.

"So now what, bro?" Rob asked a loaded question. They both knew what she was asking as they glanced at each other silently.

"Somebody knew me or was following me." Persia bit into the burger. She nodded and smiled.

"Ideas?" Rob quickly opened her eyes and looked at Lexi for a moment before closing her eyes again.

"Nobody from me. There's Ashli's ex-husband?" Lexi threw her hands up.

"No, he's married to two women now. They are about to have a kid. Nobody else cared that much about me." Persia kept eating.

"And Jade?" Rob opened her eyes.

"I heard she made her boyfriend her anchor," Persia responded. "But..."

"Yeah..." Lexi responded with a disgusted look.

"Would someone like to fill me in?" Rob shot looks at both of them.

"...Jade's secret lover...Alex." Persia said between bites.

"She blames Persia for Jade choosing her boyfriend. I think her wife left her too." Lexi shook her head. "She professed her love to Jade in front of Persia in their apartment. Only after she told her wife or fiancé, I don't know which one she was, but she told her she was leaving her for Jade.

"Oh, so ole girl blew her life up before making sure Jade wanted her..." Rob looked at Persia, "...now she's blaming you for it all?"

"I don't know. Makes sense. She was crazy. They both were. I blocked that shit out." Persia didn't even look up. She continued eating, moving on to her fries.

"That means we need to find out where...what's her name?" Rob asked Lexi.

"Alex. Her name is Alex." Lexi responded.

"Right, Alex...we need to find out where she is. Police ain't shit here. Not until we solve it first." Rob's face grew serious.

"I don't think we should. We need to protect ourselves. Maybe we should just move." Lexi panicked.

Rob jumped up from the couch, shot Persia a look in agreeance, and grabbed Lexi by her arms. "Look, we never run from a situation. Y'all build something here. I'm not going to let anyone fuck that up."

Persia smiled, "Exactly."

Lexi fell into Rob's petite arms and felt just as safe as she always did in Persia's. "I'll make a call."

"Let Rob know what you find out," Persia responded. Lexi walked over to Persia in the bed and lay next to her. "I love you. She loves you too."

"I do. I love Persia." Rob walked over to the hospital bed. "I always have. And I almost lost her. But you...you keep her safe."

Lexi looked up at Rob and watched a tear fall down Rob's cheek. She looked up at Persia; the love in her eyes while she looked at Rob was pure. She laid her head on Persia's arm and inhaled her. She felt Persia's hand caressing her back...then Rob's hand caressing her face. She looked up. They both looked down at her. Persia from the hospital bed next to her and Rob leaning on the bed towards Persia. They both had a look of anticipation...waiting for an answer to a question never verbally asked. Lexi caressed Rob's hand on her face then kissed in softly. She intertwined her fingers into Rob's and laid back on Persia. Her answer was given.

CHAPTER NINE

It didn't take long for the hospital to release Persia. She wasn't helping them keep her either. She wore the patience of the nurses and other staff at the hospital. She went straight home and continued to relax and recover in her own bed.

"Do you want anything to eat?" Rob asked Persia as she lay across the king-sized bed in her blue and purple boxer briefs, a blue sports bra, and matching socks stretched up her calf.

"Naw, I'm not really hungry. Make sure to get Lexi something. She's on the way back from the grocery store.

Lexi reached out to a friend of hers who was close to Alex. She told Lexi that Alex moved back home to stay with her sister after everything went down. She hadn't seen Alex in months. She confirmed the car Alex owned matched the one that shot at them. It was Alex. But she was gone. She must have left shortly after. No one knew where her sister lived. Most people didn't know Alex had a sister. Persia was very cautious, but Lexi wouldn't live in a box any longer. She agreed with Rob...she wasn't going to run or hide.

"Let me know when she's here so I can get the bags." Rob flipped on her back and started scrolling through social media.

"You know we have a doorman for that, right?" Persia asked.

"I don't care. It's my job to make sure she doesn't have to worry about it. And you aren't well enough to contribute to that area." Rob was chivalrous. She just looked like a fem, but she was definitely a masculine woman.

"I got you. I love that about you." Persia reached for Rob.

"What?" Rob moved next to Persia in the bed. Persia wrapped her arm around her and kissed her forehead.

"She's safe with you." Persia kissed Rob gently. Rob was intoxicated by Persia and leaned in for more. "You're safe with me."

"I know." Rob allowed herself to fall into Persia's grasp, and they kissed passionately. Persia's hand trailed up Rob's stomach, made its way under her sports bra, and found her nipple. Rob let out a soft gasp, "Shit."

Rob quickly straddled Persia and took off her sports bra. Persia appreciated the access and indulged in one nipple while she played with the other. Rob felt Persia's strap between her legs, filling her with excitement. Persia knew what she was doing. Rob quickly jumped up, standing on the bed, she pulled her boxer briefs off. Persia stared straight ahead at Rob's shaved pussy dripping wet. Rob leaned towards her and encouraged Persia to kiss her lower lips. Persia complied. She allowed Rob to ride her tongue to a couple of orgasms and didn't fight her cum dripping down her chin. Rob straddled Persia and released her strap. Persia reached into the night stand drawer, pulled out a condom, and put it on. Rob didn't want to wait; she lowered herself on Persia and took her strap into her. Every inch was ecstasy and increased her flood between her legs. When she settled on the base of the strap holding it all in her, she paused. Persia wasn't interested in a slow stroke. She palmed Rob's ass and guided her body up and down on her strap. Rob wrapped her arms around Persia's neck and gave in. She moaned and then screamed in pleasure. Sweat dripped from her body as cum dripped between her legs. Her orgasms were one right after the other...until she felt Persia's body shudder under her. She was completely engulfed in getting fucked. She completely lost track of the person fucking her. Persia let go of Rob's ass and fell back onto the headboard.

"That was...shit." Persia smiled.

"Are you finished?" Rob looked down at the fake dick still inside her. Persia grabbed her phone and started scrolling.

"Yeah, I am. Lexi is around the corner." Rob slowly got up and then quickly ran into the bathroom to clean up and get dressed.

"I'm on my way down now." Rob tossed Persia a warm, wet face cloth to clean up. She ran out of the bedroom, and Persia heard the front door close.

Rob made her way down to the lobby and waited patiently for Lexi. She chatted with the doorman as she stood at the glass entrance in basketball shorts, wife beater tank, and Jordan's staring at the street. As soon as she saw Lexi pulling up in front of the building, she broke their conversation and headed directly to her. She grabbed all the grocery bags out of the car, leaving nothing for Lexi to carry.

"Would you mind putting my car in the garage?" Lexi tossed her keys to the doorman. He never declined, and she always tipped him well. "Are you sure you can carry all that?"

"Do I look like I'm struggling?" Rob lifted her two arms filled with bags in the air almost effortlessly. The muscles in her arms, shoulders, and chest started to bulge and drew Lexi's attention.

"No, I guess not. Thanks." Lexi pressed the elevator up button and leaned on the wall peering at Rob's beautiful body, her sexy ass lips. The elevator doors opened, and they paused.

"Get your ass on the elevator so we can go," Rob laughed. "You can stare at me when we get back in the house."

"Don't flatter yourself," Lexi laughed as she watched the elevator doors close. Someone caught her eye in the lobby. They looked really familiar.

"You ok?" Rob always picked up on the changes in her moods and movements.

"Just got a weird feeling," Lexi gently shook it off.

"Let's get back inside. I don't like that." Rob directed Lexi off the elevator as soon as it opened, and she was right on her heels. She was uneasy; she trusted Lexi's intuition completely.

"OK now, babe. Give me a second." Lexi laughed as Rob pushed her towards their front door. The second elevator dinged, and they could hear the doors open and close. Rob paused. Lexi was still giggling but stopped when she felt Rob. She wasn't moving. Her breathing slowed down. "Ba..."

"Shhhhh," Rob whispered. "Someone is behind us."

Lexi's first response was to turn around in the small amount of space she had but before she could, Rob dropped the grocery bags and pushed Lexi against the door. She turned around with her hand on her gun. A stranger stood in front of them quietly, without movement.

"Where is she?" The dark figure stated.

"Alex?" Lexi asked. Tears started to flood her eyes, "You shot her?" Everything inside her body wanted to lunge at Alex. Rob's small but muscular frame was pressed against her voluptuous chocolate body; she knew not to move.

"Go inside, Lex. Now." It was a tone Lexi never heard from Rob. Her stance was different. She'd shifted into a protective mode. "Go!"

The door was unlocked. Lexi twisted the knob slowly and started to open their front door.

"Tell her to come out here," Alex stated.

"She can't do that," Rob responded. She leaned her body against Lexi to push her into the slightly opened door. Lexi reluctantly fell backward into the apartment and attempted to pull Rob with her. "You know this isn't on her."

"She took her," Alex's voice shuddered.

"How? She's not here. Jade has a boyfriend. She wants nothing to do with Persia." Rob slowly pulled the apartment door closed. "She left her for you."

"You don't know. Jade loved me. If Persia didn't..." Alex paused. "Get HER out here!"

"Ok. I will. Do you have your words set? What you're going to say?" Rob gripped her gun, releasing the safety. "If she didn't do what?"

"If she would have let her go, she would have been with me!" Alex lost focus on Rob as she reminisced on the day she lost Jade. "She fought it. I love her."

"Persia couldn't change that. It was up to Jade. She made her own decision." Rob prepared for her moment. That second, she would be able to make the necessary decision. She would take Alex's life. For Persia. For Lexi. They meant everything to her.

"Fuck You!" Alex turned to refocus on Rob and aimed her weapon at her chest. But an explosion of heat filled her gut. It pushed her back. Took her breath. For a moment, she thought she was good. Until the pain joined the heat. She touched her stomach. Blood covered her hand. She looked up at Rob. Rob still stood there with her gun in her hand, pointed directly at her. "Damn."

Rob backed into the apartment as Alex fell to her knees. Still staring at her hand covered in blood. When the door closed in front of her face, Rob broke her focus. She turned around and quickly searched for Lexi.

"Lex!" she yelled into the still apartment. Nothing. "Persia!"

The bedroom door opened slowly. Lexi peaked out and then ran out to Rob. She nestled her body into Rob's slender arms. Safe.

"I heard a gunshot." Lexi looked into Rob's eyes.

"Did you call the police?" Rob asked.

"Yes, as soon as I came in the apartment," as if her words were the cue, the sound of sirens grew in the distance. "There."

"Where's Persia?" Rob searched the doorway.

"I'm right here," Persia said as she crept into the bedroom doorway. She was still moving slowly. "Is she dead?"

"I don't know. She's down. Fucked up in the head. For real." Rob released Lexi and walked towards Persia. She could see the tears filling Rob's eyes. Rob let her face fall into Persia's neck. "I didn't..."

"You did what you had to do. You protected our family." Persia gently lifted Rob's head by her chin. "OUR family."

Rob smiled through the tears briefly, then covered her face with Persia's neck. She let out several deep sighs. Releasing the bit of guilt that still hung on her mind.

"Ma'ams, are you all okay?" A tall dark skinned police officer had entered to secure the apartment and walked into their moment.

"Yes, officer. Our family is okay. Is she?" Lexi responded.

"She's alive. On the way to the hospital now. You all are lucky." He nodded towards them. Alerted them that he would need their statement but would wait a few moments outside.

"You think you can handle us both?" Persia asked Lexi while still holding Rob in her arms.

"I think I already have," Lexi smirked, looking at them both with her arms folded. She waited for one of them to disagree. They didn't.

CHAPTER TEN

It was late into the night before everyone finally left their apartment. A few lingered in the hallway, but that didn't bother them. Their space. That's all that concerned the three of them. They laid out on the couch on top of each other. Lexi clicked through channels on the TV. Rob rubbed her nipples through her tank top. Persia cuffed Rob's neck in the crevice of her elbow. Rob rested her head on Persia's arm. Lexi finally chose a movie and fell back on Rob's stomach. She kissed Rob's hairless, sculpted stomach, then laid back on her.

"Is this our life now?" Persia asked. No one responded. They didn't move. "I'm talking to myself?"

"I feel like if we are living right now in it, then that should be the answer to the question. Which means you really shouldn't have to ask us that question. You should know. Do you know?" Lexi responded. Rob chuckled. Persia tightened her arm around Rob's neck playfully. Then kissed her on the head.

"I know," Persia laughed.

"Oh, ok. I was just making sure. You sounded a bit unsure." Lexi wasn't one to let something like that go easily.

"Lay off of her. She overanalyzes. She just needs direct confirmation sometimes. Even when it is so blatantly obvious."

Rob giggled at Lexi and turned to Persia. "Yes. This is us now. Like you said. Our family."

"Do we want it to be just the three of us?" Persia asked seriously. Lexi turned and looked at Rob. Rob returned the glance.

"Do you need more than us?" Lexi followed up.

"Romantically. No. But that's not the only way to expand a family." Persia released Rob so she could sit up and look back. The two of them looked at Persia, searching her face for some sort of idea of her seriousness. "You know...kids."

"You want kids?" Lexi asked.

"I've thought about it. I can't see there being a better family. You two are my best friends in this world. Why not?" Persia smiled.

"Lexi, we could have little ones running around." Rob chuckled at the idea. "We would need a house."

"Now we are at kids and a house?" Persia smiled. She could feel the love filling her heart spilling into her mind. This was exactly what she wanted.

"I could be convinced it's a good idea," Lexi smiled. She started kissing on Rob's stomach and pulling down the front of her shorts. Persia followed by caressing Rob's nipples. Rob submitted to Lexi pulling her shorts and underwear off. Lexi didn't waste any time. She wrapped her tongue around Rob's clit.

"I think we can come up with something," Persia laughed, then started kissing and sucking on Rob's neck.

EPILOGUE

Nobody was happy about the results with Alex, but there was nothing they could do. Alex was committed to a mental hospital for an undetermined amount of time. She was finally getting the help she truly deserved. The police tried to contact her ex to let her know what was going on, but they couldn't find her. Or she didn't want to be found. Rob had to go over what happened in that hallway more time than she would have liked. They eventually said it was self-defense and didn't charge her. Persia finally relaxed about them moving about the city on their own. Only after she equipped them both with weapons in their cars and attached them to their keys.

Persia was convinced this was the life she was trying to build. She closed their relationship, and they all agreed. Karen helped Persia propose to Rob and Lexi during their new addition photoshoot. Rob was only a few months pregnant when Persia surprised them both with engagement rings and romantic speeches. Rob cried, and of course, she blamed the pregnancy. It was exactly what they all wanted. They said yes. They planned to spend the rest of their lives celebrating their love.

It didn't take much time for Persia to find the perfect home for their almost four-member family. She made sure everyone had their own space, but there was plenty of family space. They moved quickly before Rob went into labor with their daughter. By the time they moved in, Rob was only a few days away from her due date, and Lexi was already a few months pregnant. They both had home births. Blessing their home with even more love and creativity.

Lexi gave birth to their son before their intimate wedding. Only the closest of their close friends and family were invited. Anyone who had a questioning comment about their relationship was left out. They celebrated their union on the beach until the sun came up. The five of them continued their life and love, together.

The years, the tears, the blood shed for love and happiness were not necessary but more than worth it for Persia, Rob, and Lexi. It was worth it for their own happily ever after.

Don't miss out!

Visit the website below and you can sign up to receive emails whenever Shaun J. Phree publishes a new book. There's no charge and no obligation.

https://books2read.com/r/B-A-VVFM-KXPMC

BOOKS 2 READ

Connecting independent readers to independent writers.

Did you love *Chocolate Obsession*? Then you should read *Her Mother, My Love*[1] by Shaun J. Phree!

In the spellbinding pages of "Her Mother My Love," acclaimed author Shaun J. Phree weaves a tale of love, redemption, and the indomitable spirit of human connection.

Meet Dana, a resilient 21-year-old African American lesbian stud, whose life takes an unexpected turn when she finds herself without a home after years as a devoted live-in nanny for a wealthy family. Seeking solace in her best friend and ex-girlfriend from high school, Perri, Dana's life takes a surprising twist when

---

1. https://books2read.com/u/bxBzzJ

2. https://books2read.com/u/bxBzzJ

she meets Andrea, a 19-year-old single mother with a captivating 3-year-old daughter, Trisha.

As Dana embraces her role as Trisha's nanny, a profound bond forms between them, leading to a heartfelt exploration of love and self-discovery. However, as the plot unfolds, hidden secrets and long-suppressed emotions come to the surface, setting the stage for a captivating tale of May-December love.

In the midst of this intricate web of relationships, Dana finds herself drawn to Connie, Andrea's mother, a pillar of love and support in their lives. As Dana and Connie cautiously build their relationship in secret, Perri's unspoken love for Dana simmers, adding a layer of complexity to the story.

"Her Mother My Love" delves into the raw emotions of love and family, navigating the complexities of life with authenticity and tenderness. Shaun J. Phree's masterful storytelling weaves a narrative that resonates long after the final page.

Experience the power of love's transformative journey in this heartwarming tale that celebrates diverse voices and explores the true essence of human connections. As secrets unravel and emotions collide, readers are taken on an unforgettable rollercoaster of emotions.

Unlock the captivating pages of "Her Mother My Love" and immerse yourself in a story that will touch your heart and leave you yearning for more.

"A tale of love, resilience, and the intricacies of family bonds that will stay with you long after you close the book."